FLIP

FLIP

STORY AND PICTURES BY WESLEY DENNIS

PUFFIN BOOKS

Penguin Books Ltd, Harmondsworth, Middlesex, England
Penguin Books, 625 Madison Avenue, New York, New York 10022, U.S.A.
Penguin Books Australia Ltd, Ringwood, Victoria, Australia
Penguin Books Canada Ltd, 2801 John Street, Markham, Ontario, Canada L3R 1B4
Penguin Books (N.Z.) Ltd, 182-190 Wairau Road, Auckland 10, New Zealand

First published by The Viking Press 1941
Viking Seafarer Edition published 1969
Reprinted 1971, 1972, 1974
Published in Picture Puffins 1977
Reprinted 1979, 1981

Library of Congress Cataloging in Publication Data
Dennis, Wesley.   Flip.
Summary: A colt realizes his desire to jump across the
brook following a dream in which he sprouts silvery wings.
[1. Horses—Fiction] I. Title.
PZ7.D4282F12 [E] 77-2563
ISBN 0-14-050203-3

Printed in the United States of America
by Rae Publishing Co., Inc., Cedar Grove, New Jersey
Set in Caslon

To Linda and Karen

Flip was born.

His home was a large farm in Kentucky with miles and miles of split rail fences and big trees. A clear, sparkling stream wound in and out among the green fields. Flip wanted to get out there and play.

It wasn't long before his mother was teaching him to walk and then to run. Flip thought this was great fun.

Every day that they came to the stream Flip's mother would jump lightly over it and back again. Flip thought this a beautiful sight and wished that he could do it.

He could do plenty of other things. He could kick and buck and fairly twist himself inside out, or run circles around his mother, sometimes nipping her and pulling her tail.

To get away from these antics, his mother would often jump over the brook to graze. Flip would be left whinnying on the other side. "Oh, if I could only jump as she does!" he would sigh.

He tried and tried. Sometimes he would run right up to the edge and stop suddenly.

Other times he wouldn't stop soon enough and would fall in.

When he did jump, he always landed in the water instead of on the opposite bank.

Because he couldn't jump the stream it soon became the one thing in the world that he wished to do.

One day he tried so hard and so long that he tired himself out and fell asleep wishing—wishing that he could jump the brook like his mother —perhaps higher and further!

As he slept, he dreamed.

Suddenly he felt his shoulders itching. He looked around. He had grown a pair of beautiful silvery wings.

He was so excited that his knees knocked. His hair stood on end.

He thought: "With these wings I can jump over anything I please! That haystack should be easy."

It was such a success that he didn't want to stop a minute. On he went over the split rail fences.

A little more effort and he was saying "Hello" to the iron horse that told which way the wind was blowing. Flip was sorry for him. "He can only run in a circle," he thought; "I can fly anywhere!"

This was the greatest fun he had ever imagined. He wanted only one thing more—that his friends on the farm should see him jumping higher and further than any horse had ever jumped before. So he swooped down over the barn.

Piggly-Woof saw him coming and was so scared that his tail uncurled, stood up straight, and stayed that way.

Old Scratch-and-Cackle, seeing on the ground the shadow of a flying horse, thought the world was coming to an end. She fled to the nearest sunflower and gathered her chicks beneath her. But not one of them could keep his eyes from the skies.

Swish, the cat, jumped on the back of Willy-the-Goat to get a better view.

But Willy was so frightened that he ran full speed ahead and caught his horns in the fence and sent the cat sailing through the air.

Flip was enjoying all this very much but he did wish that a big horsefly droning and buzzing around him would leave him alone.

But it didn't leave him alone and Flip snapped at it.

As he moved, he woke up.

And there, right in front of him, was the same brook that he had tried so many times to jump. It would be easy now with his silver wings!

So he backed up to get a good running start—

AND CLEARED THE BROOK, WITH

PLENTY OF ROOM TO SPARE.

He was so thrilled to have finally jumped it that he looked back to admire once again his silvery wings, but to his astonishment they were gone!

GREAT SCOTT—he had jumped the brook without the wings!